Strawberry

HILL

Illustrated by Frances Espanol
Authors Photo by Cynthia Sheila Bankhead II

To order additional copies of this book, contact:
Xlibris
844-714-8691
www.Xlibris.com
Orders@Xlibris.com

ISBN:	Softcover	978-1-6641-7102-2
	EBook	978-1-6641-6865-7

Print information available on the last page

Rev. date: 06/14/2021

Strawberry Hill

NANCY T. CURRY

Long ago in the forest of Green Horn, where the mist of jasper fog and the waters of Lemon's Creek and the smell of cupcakes and cream dance around a little girl named Dakota. That's me. The wind would blow and the flowers would bloom, the trees would be filled with honeysuckles and gumdrops, and the grass soft as cotton candy. What a way to spend the summer at Strawberry Hill with my grandparents, Mr. and Mrs. Hill.

It all began when I was, oh, I'II say around six years old, my parents would put me on a train and my adventure would begin, of course, not without my big brother Jessie and sister Kylie. Mom would make sack lunches while Dad attended to the luggage. Dad would comfort Mom as she waves as the train headed off. I would be so excited my face was blushed like the color of a candy apple. When I see my grandparents out the window standing, waiting on the side of the train, off I would fly into their arms. Grandma smells like sugar cookies and Grandpa with his long white beard smells like his old pipe that I loved so well.

"Hello, kids!"

"Hello!" Jessie and Kylie reply with their arms open wide. Jessie would place the luggage in the trunk and off to Strawberry Hill we go as we pulled up to the house that sits on miles and miles of strawberry land and passes through the fields. Beyond the sky was a land that only kids dream of, where mystical magic and imagination become a reality.

As we enter the house, I can see Grandma's cupcakes with my favorite topping—candy sprinkles!

"Thanks, Grandma! You rock!"

"You're welcome, little one, but not before supper."

"Yes, ma'am. May I go out to the strawberry field?"

"Of course, you may. Be back in time to wash up for supper."

"Yes, ma'am," I reply. Out the door I go with my sack across my back, full of crayons, paper, pencils, and markers, and, of course, my imagination.

Time goes by; its 3:00 p.m. Time to head back for supper. I arrive just in time. Grandpa is waiting at the front door with his pipe in his hand.

"Wash up, young lady."

"Yes, sir."

Jessie, Kylie, and I had always been remarkable and polite children. After supper, Kylie and Grandma wash the dishes as I get ready for bed after a long day of excitement. Good night.

CYNTHIA'S
Warm Bread
&
Jam

The next morning, I wake up at around 6:00 a.m. to the smell of Grandma's cooking and Grandpa's pipe. I just know that this is going to be an awesome morning, all washed up and ready for breakfast. Yum, here I come! My grandparents are the best—full of love, joy, and excitement and they give the best advice too.

For example, Grandma would always say, "Do all the good when you can, while you can, and goodwill always comes back around to you." Now Grandpa, on the other hand, would say, "Eat awhile, live awhile"—how funny is that! Grandpa loves his snacks in between every meal and one just before bedtime, with a pipe in his hand and his long white beard hanging down from his face. With a great sense of humor and a vivid imagination, Grandpa would always smile. He would have the most awesome stories to tell. Grandma smells like a fresh bakery that just opened in springtime. Her cheeks are the color of a soft red rose; her laughter would brighten up your day. There was nothing that she wouldn't do for her family and others, just like Mommy.

My grandparents met in a small town called Boysenberry on a rainy day, while heading out to Cynthia's Warm Bread and Jams. This was the ideal place where the townspeople of Ireland would rest their minds after a long day's work—sit and talk awhile as the fresh homemade bread would fill the walls of thirty-one flavors of homemade jams. As Grandpa sat and awaited his delight, he couldn't help but notice from across the room the most beautiful woman of all Ireland. Her face was like an angel and her smile was breathtaking. He could not believe that such a woman was sitting alone with tears falling down her rosy cheeks. Being the gentleman that he was raised to be, he walked over and said to his darling, "Would you like some Bread and Jam?" He was so nervous his knees were knocking together as if it was a cold winter's night. She smiled at him and began to wipe away the tears from her eyes, and from that day forward, they have been happily married for over fifty years.

Grandpa started growing strawberries early in his days, with the best homegrown fertilizer in the world. The strawberries are red and sweet to the taste. People come from all over the world just for the great taste of Mr. Hill's strawberries. So Grandpa took his last name and added the word strawberry, placed the two words together and came about the name Strawberry Hill. Right to this day, people from all over the world come up just to get that great taste of strawberries, and that's how it all began.

Jessie and Kylie finally arrive for breakfast. Grandpa says in his Ireland voice, "Top of the morning to yeah! Kids, did you sleep well?"

"Yes, sir, great!"

"Go into the kitchen and get a bit to eat." And off they go.

"Good morning, Grandma."

"Well, good morning, sleepy heads. Did you sleep well?"

"Yes, ma'am!"

As Grandma prepares our plates starting off with a large glass of orange juice, strawberry banana waffles, scrambled eggs, and homemade sausages from Jo Meat Market.

After breakfast, I pull up a chair to help Grandma wash the dishes, which Kylie and I would often take turns doing. Time goes by and its time to head out. I gather up my things and up under the old willow tree, I would go to my favorite place to be. Nature is beautiful with the trees a-blowing and the wind a-whistling. I begin to create a world of magic with my crayons, markers, and, of course, my imagination of beautiful creeks, green grass, bright yellow sun, cottages throughout the village, rainbows, waterfalls, talking trees, berry fairies, and the fairy people. You can always tell when it's time to head home. The wind is calm, the air is still, and the night is peaceful across the land. Time to head back before my family comes a-looking. Being the youngest, they're overprotective of me, you know.

.35¢
.60¢
Jo's
Meat Market

It's never a dull moment around the Hill family. Each day is like waking up to the best parks, ever full of excitement. My father is the baby boy. His name is William Hill. He is the youngest of fourteen children. Can you believe that? My grandparents had fourteen children, ten boys and four girls. my mother is also the baby girl. Her name is Annabelle, and she comes from a family where the girls overpower the boys—five girls and two boys. I would love to tell you how my parents came about, but that would be for another story.

Each morning at around 4:00 a.m., us chicks would wake up and put on our overalls, an old shirt, and boots and grab a basket and a large hat to keep the "hot" sun from beaming down our faces. We then head out to the strawberry field only to pick the best red strawberries in the world from the bushels. As for me, I would eat awhile and work awhile. Grandpa would have the tractor waiting and us little people would be a hauling.

Each night, Mom would call with hugs and kisses through the phone. We have never been away from our parents, not even for a moment; this is the first. Our parents thought it would be nice for us to come down this summer alone until they arrived . . . and the phone calls never stopped coming.

We are off to Cynthia's Warm Bread and Jams, the place where my grandparents first met. It's standing room only but worth the wait. Grandma wanted the family to taste the delicious tropical mango jam. Off to the next stop: Jo's Meat Market, what a treat! You could smell the fresh jerky for miles. I couldn't wait to walk through the doors. Ms. Jo would always have a nice bag of beef and turkey jerky just waiting for me. Grandma would get three pounds of fresh sausages, three whole chickens, four pounds of ground beef, three pounds of corn beef—after all, this is the best meat market in town. Jessie would unload as Kylie and Grandma prepare for the carving of the chickens, while placing the food in the coolers. I would be somewhere in between helping, with a beef jerky in my hand, preparing for the family gatherings held throughout the month. We would laugh awhile and eat awhile. What fun! There is nothing like family, the Hill family, that is. Time goes by and the night is peaceful. I believe I'II go out and rest my head upon the stars tonight. I grabbed my blanket and my fluffy pillow and head out the back door only to see my family as well, resting amongst the stars. A day is gone by and I didn't get the chance to go on my adventure. Yet today was a good day shopping with Grandma.

"Top of the morning to you, Grandma! What's for breakfast? Need any help?"

"No, darling, not this time. I'm preparing something a little light—'hot' strawberry oatmeal, toast and jam, milk or orange juice and, of course, your grandpa's 'hot' tea."

"Thanks, Grandma, love you."

"Oh, you're welcome, little one. Go and wake the others and don't leave out your grandpa."

I laugh. "Yes, ma'am, right away." I head down the hallway with a loud voice to wake up everyone. Grandma laughs; she knew that I was up to something being awake before Grandpa. And that's never happened. You could hear everyone's feet hit the floor while Grandpa wakes up from a loud snore. I tell you, he sounds like a bear at times.

It's a lovely morning. Everyone is sitting around the table, except Grandpa.

"Oh, don't worry a bit. He'll be a-coming. Moving a little slow this morning, are we?"

"Yes, darling, I believe so."

"Now that wouldn't happen to be from all of those teacakes and milk from last night's snack, would it, dear?"

“I believe so.” With smiles on our faces, everyone bursts with a chuckle and then a laugh.

“Shall we say grace before the food gets cold?” It’s Jessie’s turn to say grace over the food. You see, we each take turns saying grace in the Hills’ home; it’s a must.

I often peek at Jessie because he can be longwinded at times. I often wonder, where does he get the wind from to keep the words a-coming? If we wait on him, breakfast will be freezing cold.

Breakfast is over, and its time for me to head out to the field.

“Not so fast, young lady,” Grandma said. “Come back here and help wash up the dishes.

“Yes, ma’am,” I said in a cute little voice. Now that the kitchen is all tidy, “May I go out to the field, Grandma?”

“Yes! You may go out the door.”

I run across Strawberry Hill through the trees and the tall green grass. The smell of lemon waterfalls, a scent that I have never smelled before, blows in the wind. It is peaceful sitting under my willow tree. I couldn’t help but notice as I began my drawing a door appeared. I jumped up off the ground, saying to myself, This is new.

Curiosity gets the best of me every time; as I approach the door, the smell of lemon waterfalls, honeysuckles, and so many other aromas enhanced my attention. And just as I placed my hand on the doorknob, my sister Kylie calls out to me, "Dakota, Dakota!" and out of the forest I go running. While I was running, all I could think about was that door.

"Wow, Kylie, why were you calling me like that? You startled me!"

"You startled?" said Kylie. "That's a first." Into the house we go.

"Well, hello, little one," said Grandpa. "You look as if you came across something."

"It's the strangest thing, Grandpa," I said. "I saw a door in the forest over by my willow tree. I've never seen anything like that before."

Grandpa chuckled, saying to himself, I was wondering when that was going to show up. As a kid, I too had such an adventure. There has always been magic in the forest of Ireland, and the Hill family just so happen to be sitting on a piece of that land.

"How was your day, sweetheart?" asked Grandma.

"It was adventurous and mysterious," I said.

"Is that so," said Grandma.

"Yes, ma'am," I said. "Today, I saw a door over by the willow tree. It was so exciting."

Grandma smiled and gave a nod as if she knew of this magical place. All is well in Strawberry Hill; goodnight all.

“Good morning, fine people of the Hills’ home. Dakota, you’re up bright-eyed and bushy-tail this morning. Will you be heading off to the fields?”

“Yes, ma’am. May I?”

“Of course you may.”

Over by the willow tree I go, as I pull out my paper and crayons and new markers Grandpa brought for me from the local store around town. Grandma knew that this would be an adventurous day so she packed a lunch full of my favorites: a grilled cheese sandwich, an apple, chips, and a juice box. Trying not to think about the door and yet I found myself approaching this tiny door, curious as to how to enter in. Looking around for the key, I stumbled across a mailbox covered with orange and yellow flowers, and inside was the key that will unlock the magic. And just as I placed my hands on the door, a loud voice from the field is heard, “Dakota! Dakota!” Kylie yells out and I took off running, scaring me to pieces. I placed my hands on my forehead saying, “Kylie, why must you call me like that?”

Kylie replied with laughter, “Mom and Dad are here!”

I leap into the air with excitement. I have so much to say to them. With arms open wide, I grab them both around the neck and hold them tight. Tonight, the sky is full of laughter with a smiley face on the moon. Tonight was a grand night. Good night.

The next morning, I awakened to breakfast being prepared. Of course, Mom and Grandma were up at the crack of dawn while Grandpa, with his pipe in his hand, along with Dad, are outside enjoying the morning dew. It's good to see Mom and Grandma in the kitchen together. Mom makes the best apple strudels with a pinch of vanilla cream over the top. As everyone pulls up to the table, Dad gives thanks. Grandpa and I peek out the corner of our eyes to see if Dad was going to be longwinded. You don't get a grandpa like mine every day. Breakfast is over and I zoom out the front door.

Heading to the willow tree, I had to get a jump start on opening the mystical door. The closer I got, the stronger the aroma became the smell of lemon waterfalls and honeysuckles strawberries. And the more I pulled back the vines, I just couldn't believe my eyes. It was as if I was stepping into my drawing. "Am I dreaming?"

There was a land of little people made of strawberries. There were lemon waterfalls and marshmallow clouds, and the grass was like green apple cotton candy. I am surrounded in a village of strawberry; little people whose houses are made of strawberry shortcake and whose roads are made of gumdrops songs. Laughter fills the air as I stand with excitement as if I have already seen this place. Once upon a time, when I was just a baby, our friendship grew over time during the summer months spent at my grandparents' house. Well, the summer has come to an end and it's time to head back home. It's always a pleasure visiting my grandparents and my friends in the Land of Strawberries. As to what happens in the Land of Strawberries, that would be for another story, my friends.

About the Author

Nancy T. Curry grew up in Grand Rapids, Michigan. She started writing when she was only thirteen years old. The first poem she wrote was called "The Colors of My Scales." By the time, she turned thirty, she had written four children's books and two poetry books. She received a certificate in child psychology while working on her associate degree in sociology at Muskegon Community College. A church announcer, a youth developmental specialist, a poet, and author of the book *Melody of a Lovebird Song*, Nancy is a mother of two; and she had learned in entirely different ways. She is full of life, love, and happiness with a vivid imagination and an appetite for sweet strawberries. Her adventure has just begun. You can reach her at nancycurry69@gmail.com.

About the Book

In the land of strawberries, Dakota finds herself standing inside of her drawings. A place where imagination of lemon waterfalls, marshmallow clouds, green apple cotton candy trees, gumdrops, and the king and queen of Strawberry Land comes to life. It's magical what a box of crayons, markers, and paper can do.

Printed in the United States
by Baker & Taylor Publisher Services